Zoomer Field Notes

Teeth

goatrilla

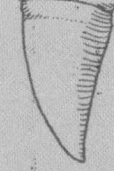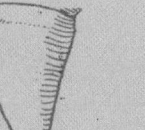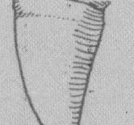
polar cow

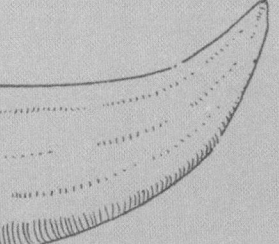
dogephant

shicken

pigcock

norsodile

libbit

shiger

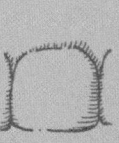
norsodile

Poo

libbit

norsodile

duckaroo

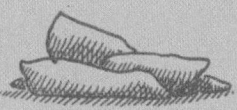
shicken

shiger

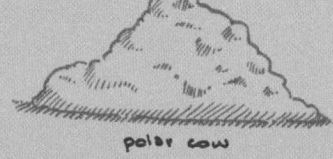
polar cow

pigcock

goatrilla

givapooster

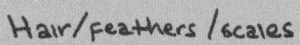
dogephant

Hair/feathers/scales

goatrilla

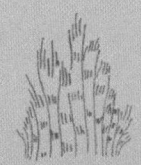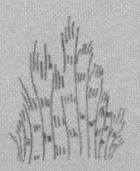
polar cow

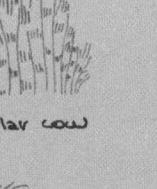
shiger

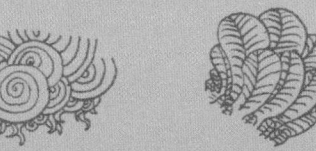
shicken

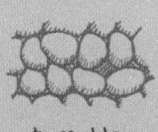
norsodile

pigcock

dogephant

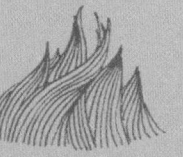
givapooster

libbit

For Tom,
the original zoomer.

First published in Great Britain in 2015 by Andersen Press Ltd.,
20 Vauxhall Bridge Road, London SW1V 2SA.
This paperback edition first published in 2016 by Andersen Press Ltd.
Text copyright © Ana de Moraes, 2015.
Illustration copyright © Thiago de Moraes, 2015.
The rights of Ana de Moraes and Thiago de Moraes to be identified
as the author and illustrator of this work have been asserted by them
in accordance with the Copyright, Designs and Patents Act, 1988.
All rights reserved.
Printed and bound in Singapore.

1   3   5   7   9   10   8   6   4   2

British Library Cataloguing in Publication Data available.
ISBN 978 1 78344 215 7

The ZOOMERS' Handbook

Ana & Thiago de Moraes

ANDERSEN PRESS

This is *not* a handbook for zookeepers.

Zookeepers look after monkeys, elephants and lions. That's easy.

This is *not* a handbook for farmers.

Farmers look after chickens, cows and pigs.
Anyone can do that.

This is a handbook for *Zoomers*.
Zoomers look after very special beasts . . .

Take the goatrilla for example. He likes to climb and he likes to swing from trees. Remember to feed him at least 10 cans of bananas a day. He loves to eat cans.

**This
is the
polar cow, a
very practical animal.
If you feed it strawberries
and get it to dance around before
milking time, it makes ice cream!**

The shiger
is grandma's
favourite
animal.
Its stripy
wool makes
the nicest
jumpers.

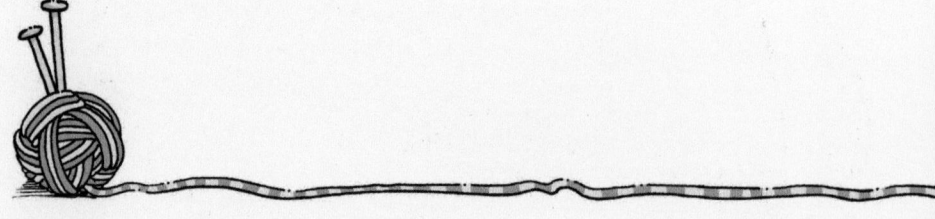

The shicken lays delicious eggs,

but letting it eat corn from your hand is not a good idea.

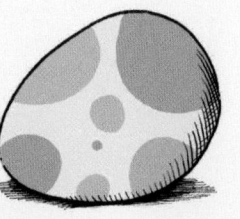

The horsodile is the best ride when you need

to get somewhere fast, even if it's underwater.

The pigcock is one of the most beautiful animals on earth – at least in theory.

Few people have seen its feathers, as they are often covered in mud.

**The dogephant
loves to play.
But don't let it
jump on you:
it weighs a ton.**

The girafooster will get you up bright and early. It spots the sun

from way up high, as soon as it starts to rise.

nest,

a   it

need   keeps

The   doesn't

duckaroo

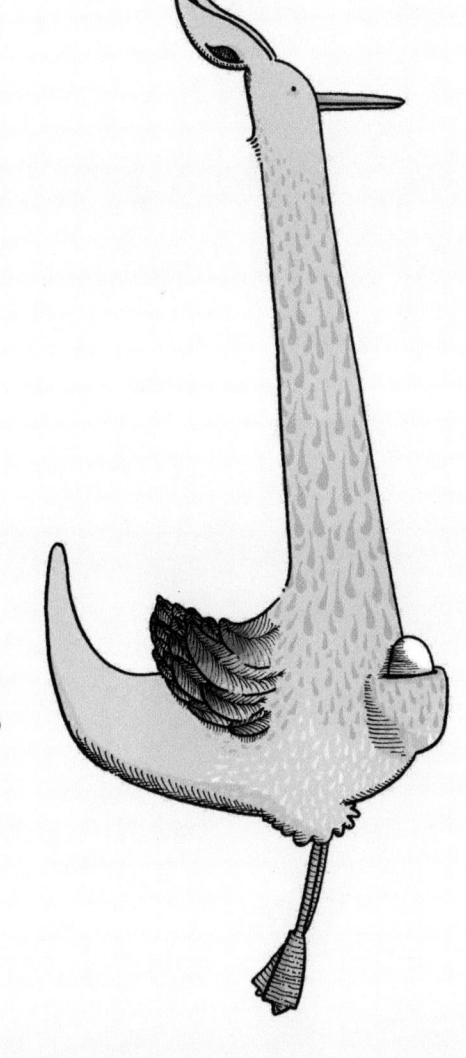

instead.

pouch

its

the   in

eggs

Finally, beware of the libbit: it may be small,

but it likes to be treated like a king.

**Now that you've met all the animals,
you know what it takes to be a Zoomer.**

It's time to get to work!

Zoomer Field Notes

duckaroo hatching

newborn duckaroo

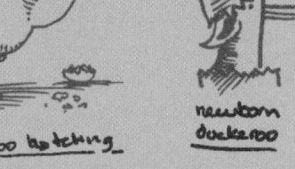

Gostrilla family
Mum, dad & three month old baby

— adult duckaroo leap —

Front

back

food

polar cow walking

polar cow standing

polar cow dancing

shicken in nest

horsadile & heron

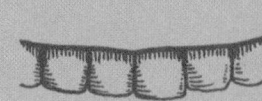

teeth

shicken chicks

noss

ear

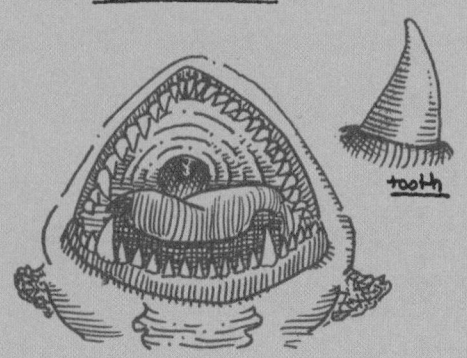

tooth

givafooster

giraffe

elephant

polar bera

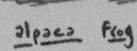

alpaca

frog

Zoomer Field Notes

polar cow ice cream

polar cow sleeping

libbit roaring

tail

crest

girafcooler family

polar cow footprint

cubs

paw

egg

footprint

chick

libbit hole

footprint

foot

tiger stretching

jumper

hat

socks

dogephant & birds

paw

paw print

tiger wool

nose

tail

tusk

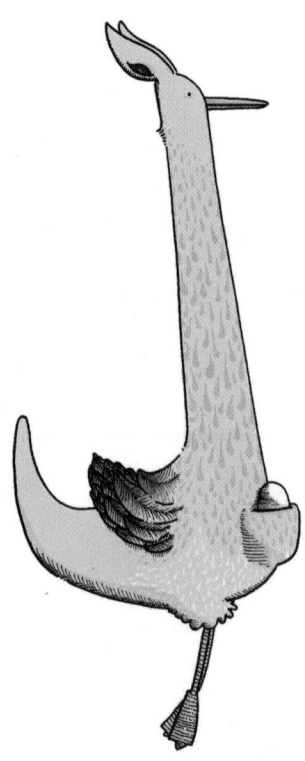